THE KING'S GIFT

A tribute to His Majesty the late King Hussein of Jordan

from Her Majesty Queen Rania Al-Abdullah

Created by Her Majesty Queen Rania Al-Abdullah
Text: Ghada Ramzi Muasher
Illustrations: Angel Dominguez

First published in 2000 by Michael O'Mara Books Limited,
9 Lion Yard, Tremadoc Road, London SW4 7NQ

Copyright © 2000 The Office of Her Majesty Queen Rania Al-Abdullah of Jordan
Illustrations copyright © 2000 The Office of Her Majesty Queen Rania Al-Abdullah
and Angel Dominguez
Text by Ghada Ramzi Muasher
Designed and edited by David Sinden

A CIP catalogue record for this book is available from the British Library

ISBN 1-85479-573-2
Jordanian Deposit no. (1999/12/2314)

Manufactured and printed in Dubai

Foreword
by
Her Majesty Queen Rania Al-Abdullah

In the years ahead, historians and scholars will, no doubt, write about the legacy of the late King Hussein. They will describe at length his achievements and the impact he had not only upon our nation, but indeed upon the entire world. They will speak of a leader who had vision, courage, honour, and an infinite compassion for all of his people. Their words will be inspiring, captivating and yet somehow incomplete.

The true measure of the greatness of King Hussein lies not merely in his accomplishments, but in the nature of the man himself. I feel truly blessed and privileged to have had the opportunity to know such an extraordinary character close up. I saw the wise and loving father. I saw the kind and nurturing grandfather. I saw a man with an endless capacity for caring – a man who rejoiced in the joy of others. I also saw a leader who embraced his nation as a father would his own family. There is no doubt in my mind that the legacy King Hussein left behind is a wellspring that we as individuals, and we as nations, can draw upon for ever.

The King's Gift is a modern fable that tells the story of a curious young schoolgirl who is guided by the King in an exciting search for the royal crown. The girl eventually finds the crown but in a form very different to the one she had originally imagined. In fact, it comes to her in the form of a gift – one that is very special indeed. It is this gift that I would like children everywhere to understand and remember.

What an exciting day! The King was coming to our school to see our spring play. I was so happy when the headmistress told me that I had been chosen to offer him a bouquet of flowers!

I waited anxiously for him to arrive. I imagined him walking down the red carpet wearing his sparkling golden crown and royal cape.

Parents, teachers and children stood waiting in the big hall. I stared at the royal guards as they marched in. My heart started beating faster. Soon I would shake hands with the King!

The welcoming cheers of the crowd echoed in the playground. Everyone around me applauded. It was time for me to present the bouquet. I searched for the man wearing a crown, but could not see him anywhere.

Just then I spotted a man with coloured badges on his chest and a small golden crown on the front of his hat. I was about to hand him the flowers when the headmistress pulled me back.

"He is not the King," she whispered, and she gently turned me around to face a line of men in suits.

So which one is the King? I thought.

Frantically I searched among them. Not one of them wore a crown.

I was so nervous my legs were shaking. I was about to fall when two strong arms reached out and steadied me. They were the arms of a man. I looked into his face. He was a young, friendly looking man.

I held out the flowers to him. He took them and smiled.

I knew he must be the King.

"I'm so sorry, I thought you would be wearing a crown!" I said.

He laughed and in a deep calm voice said, "I am, but it isn't easy to see."

I looked at him a little confused. "What do you mean, Your Majesty?" I asked. "I mean you have to search for it," the King replied.

He reached into his pocket and pulled out a small pair of golden wings.

"Take these," he said. "They will help you find the crown."

I was waiting for an explanation but the King gave none. He looked ahead at the stage.

I stared at the golden wings in my hand. Two streaks of light flashed from their centre, right into my eyes.

The purple curtains opened and I found myself in the peaceful garden of a beautiful palace. The King turned towards me and said, "Are you ready to fly over the land to look for the crown?"

"But how, how can I fly?"
"You have the golden wings," the King replied.
Suddenly the golden wings grew into two wings like those of a falcon. With his gentle hands, the King fastened the wings to my outstretched arms.
"Don't be afraid, my child. You will not fall," he said. "I will be with you wherever you are."

I swiftly took off into the clear blue sky.

I gazed below at the ancient ruins, wide-open sand dunes, green mountains, valleys, rivers and seas.

Could the crown be on top of a mountain, or under the sand, or deep in the sea? I wondered.

I landed in the middle of the desert. Beautiful music filled the air. Bedouins were dancing joyfully in a large circle.

I walked over to a group of women sitting on the ground weaving rugs on wooden looms.

"I am searching for a crown," I said. "Have you seen one?"

"Not here," a woman replied. "But you are welcome to stay with us until you find it."

I walked towards a tent, and was astonished to see the King inside. He was sitting among the elders of the tribe, drinking their coffee and sharing stories with them.

I ran to him and exclaimed, "I cannot find the crown!"

The King just smiled, then stood up to go. He shook hands with the tribesmen and thanked them for their hospitality.

One of the elders of the tribe handed him a piece of brass as a gift. The King thanked him and passed it to me. "Take this," he said. "Hold on to your wings and you will find the crown."

I took the piece of brass, flapped my wings and took off again over the sand dunes.

High in the sky, I noticed that the clouds were turning grey. The winds were blowing against me. My wings were quivering and I began to lose my balance. A bolt of lightning struck and pierced my wings.

I was terrified. I felt myself slipping away, downwards, downwards.

Finally I landed on the roof of a tall building.

I walked down a flight of stairs and found myself in a hospital full of wounded soldiers. There were men everywhere, hurt and in pain. I was relieved to see the King there. He was standing among the wounded, comforting them.

One young soldier began to speak. "Your Majesty, please accept this from me," he said to the King. "My grandfather gave it to me." The young soldier took from around his neck a blue bead threaded on a string, and handed it to the King.

The King was touched. "Thank you," he said. "I will cherish it."

I walked up to the King, sobbing. "I cannot fly any more," I told him. "My wings are broken."

The King unthreaded the blue bead from the string and put it into my hands. "Take this bead and look after it," he said. "I will fix your wings with the string."

I felt the King tying my wings back together. He put his hand on my shoulder. "Keep flying," he said. "You will find the crown."

I took off again and soared high above the rooftops. The gentle breeze carried me like a leaf over mountains and a sprawling city.

I saw houses, schools, factories and airports spread beneath me, and felt myself being drawn towards a grassy square among the buildings of a university.

I glided swiftly downwards.

The King was standing in the square, addressing the graduates.

"Man is our greatest asset," he said.

Everyone applauded.

One of the graduates walked towards the King and handed him a tiny book. The King was delighted. He passed it to me, saying, "You must be strong. You still have more to discover."

Then he gestured to me to fly again.

I flew north over wide plains and old castles until I reached a green valley alongside a river. Red poppies and wild daisies decorated the roadside. Black irises stood tall among the rocks. The smell of lemon blossoms beckoned me lower, and I landed in the orchard of a small village farm.

As I walked through the orchard, I saw a young woman gathering oranges. "Excuse me, I'm looking for a crown," I said to her.

The woman peeled an orange, handed it to me and told me to follow her into a stone house on the farm.

Inside the farmhouse a group of villagers had gathered around the King. The King was drinking their mint tea and listening to their plans for the harvest. An old man walked over, carrying a baby pine tree in a pot. He offered it to the King as a gift.

"Thank you," the King said, "but we must plant this tree if this place is to stay green and beautiful."

The King knelt down and with his strong hands dug a small hole in the ground. Gently he placed the tree into the hole, covering its fine roots with soil and pouring water over them from a jug.

As the King stood up to admire the tree, a single cone fell from one of its branches. He picked it up, handed it to me and said, "Take this pine cone. Now fly south and discover the abundant waters of the sea."

I headed south above sandstone hills, valleys, dunes and a city carved in stone. I flew over purple mountains until, sparkling below me, were the crystal waters of a calm sea.

I landed on a quiet sandy beach.

The King was with a group of men preparing the nets to go fishing. He stood up and waved to me.

Together we walked along the beach where we met a boy filling glass bottles with sand. The King stopped to admire the different shapes of coloured glass.

"This one is my favourite," said the boy. He handed the King a piece of green glass blown in the shape of a fish.

The King was pleased. He passed me the glass fish, saying, "Look through the glass and tell me what you see."

I held the glass fish to my eyes. I was amazed to see myself soaring across borders, over oceans to faraway lands.

In every land the King was there, greeting people who spoke different languages. They all shook hands with him.

"Now it is time to return to the palace," the King said to me. "Keep the glass fish with the other gifts. Soon you will find the crown."

With one strong flap of my wings, I took off from the water's edge. I flew over the sea, the purple mountains, the city carved in stone, the valleys, the orchards, the poppies, the ancient castles, the rivers, the universities, the factories, the hospitals, the green mountains and the golden desert, until I landed in the peaceful garden of the King's palace.

The King took my hand.
"I want you to meet the children who live in my home," he said.
I watched as children ran from all corners of the garden to greet the King with bouquets of flowers, balloons and pictures they'd drawn. A small girl hugged the King and handed him an olive branch.

"One day," the King said to me, "in a city on a hill, children will be playing together quite happily in a garden full of olive trees."
"But Your Majesty, what about the crown?" I asked.

The King looked at me with kind eyes. "You've already found the crown," he said, "in each place we've visited, in each person we've met and in all the gifts we've been given. Just piece them together."

I placed the gifts in front of me and gazed at them: the piece of brass, the blue bead, the book, the pine cone, the glass fish and the olive branch. "I don't understand," I said.

"My child," the King explained. "The brass is the foundation on which dreams are built, the blue bead is the faith that will guide you, the book is the knowledge that will give you wisdom and strength, the pine cone is the seed of love that will nurture you, the glass is the vision of a better future, and the olive branch is the peace that makes all the other gifts endure."

"But how is this a crown?" I asked him.

"Look carefully at the brass," the King said.

I stared at the rectangular piece of brass. It had four holes in one of its sides. Each hole had a different shape: one was round, one square, one triangular and one oval. I looked at the gifts in front of me.

It was a puzzle!

Picking up the blue bead, I fitted it into the round hole. Next I placed the tiny book into the square hole. The pine cone slotted into the triangular hole, and the glass fish lay in the oval hole.

The King handed me the olive branch. "Now take this," he said, "and tie them all together."

Delicately I laced the gifts into the brass with the olive branch, weaving the treasures together in a circle.

When I saw what I had made, I jumped up and down.

"I've found the crown! I've found the crown!"

The King smiled. With his gentle hands, he placed the crown on to my head. The gifts sparkled like jewels and the brass shone like gold. I was beaming with joy.

"So now you've found it," the King said. "You've found the crown, and now I must leave."

He began to walk away from the palace.

"Please don't go!" I cried....

Then the purple curtains closed and the audience applauded.
I felt the King's hand on my shoulder.
"Did you enjoy it?" he said to me.
"Very much," I told him. I stood up to give him back his wings.
"You may keep them," he said. "They're yours now." He proudly pinned the golden wings on to my chest. "My dear child," he continued, "I must leave you now, but I know you are in good hands."

The King stood up from his chair and strode out through the hall towards the school gate. His strong arms were at his sides and his head was held high.
I ran after him.
The Bedouins, the soldiers, the graduates, the villagers, the children and the people from towns and cities were all there, scattering flowers along his path.
He turned back and waved to me.
"Look after your wings," he said, "they are my gift to you."